At the Beach

By Patricia M. Stockland

Cuyahoga Falls
Library
Cuyahoga Falls, Ohio

Illustrated by Amy Bailey Muehlenhardt

Special thanks to our advisers for their expertise:

Adria F. Klein, Ph.D.
Professor Emeritus, California State University
San Bernardino, California

Rosemary G. Palmer, Ph.D.
Department of Literacy, College of Education
Boise State University

PICTURE WINDOW BOOKS
Minneapolis, Minnesota

Levels for *Read-it!* Readers

- Familiar topics
- Frequently used words
- Repeating patterns

- New ideas
- Larger vocabulary
- Variety of language structures

- Challenges in ideas
- Expanded vocabulary
- Wide variety of sentences

- More complex ideas
- Extended vocabulary range
- Expanded language structures

A Note to Parents and Caregivers:

Read-it! Readers are for children who are just starting on the amazing road to reading. These beautiful books support both the acquisition of reading skills and the love of books.

The RED LEVEL presents familiar topics using common words and repeating sentence patterns.

The BLUE LEVEL presents new ideas using a larger vocabulary and varied sentence structure.

The YELLOW LEVEL presents more challenging ideas, a broad vocabulary, and wide variety in sentence structure.

The GREEN LEVEL presents more complex ideas, an extended vocabulary range, and expanded language structures.

When sharing a book with your child, read in short stretches, pausing often to talk about the pictures. Have your child turn the pages and point to the pictures and familiar words, and be sure to reread favorite stories or parts of stories.

There is no right or wrong way to share books with children. Find time to read with your child, and pass on the legacy of literacy.

Adria F. Klein, Ph.D.
Professor Emeritus
California State University
San Bernardino, California

Managing Editor: Catherine Neitge
Creative Director: Terri Foley
Editor: Christianne Jones
Designer: Jaime Martens
Page production: Picture Window Books
The illustrations in this book were prepared digitally.

Picture Window Books
5115 Excelsior Boulevard
Suite 232
Minneapolis, MN 55416
877-845-8392
www.picturewindowbooks.com

Printed in the United States of America.

Library of Congress Cataloging-in-Publication Data
Stockland, Patricia M.
At the beach / by Patricia M. Stockland ; illustrated by Amy Bailey Muehlenhardt.
p. cm. — (Read-it! readers)
Summary: A family goes to the beach for a day full of fun and adventure.
ISBN 1-4048-0651-2 (hardcover)
[1. Beaches—Fiction.] I. Muehlenhardt, Amy Bailey, 1974- ill. II. Title. III. Series.
PZ7.S865At 2004
[E]—dc22   2004007359

We can do so many things
at the beach!

I dig for shells.

Mom takes a nap.

I splash in the salty sea.

Mom and Dad swim.

I spy a lighthouse and lots of boats.

Dad holds me high, so I
can see like a seagull.

I make a new friend.

We play catch.

Her mom yells for more sunblock!

We say good-bye.

I am hungry, so Dad buys
me ice cream.

Mom is warm, so she buys a big hat.

We look for treasure.

I find an egg.

Dad finds a jug.

I find a log.

Mom finds a crab.

Everybody run!

The crab is mad!

We are safe!

We build a sand castle.

Everyone helps.

Mom and Dad are tired.

Mom says it's time to go!

The water waves as we
say good-bye.

We did so many things
at the beach!

Levels for *Read-it!* Readers

**Read-it! Readers help children practice early reading
skills with brightly illustrated stories.**

 Red Level: Familiar topics with frequently used words and
repeating patterns.

I Am in Charge of Me by Dana Meachen Rau
Let's Share by Dana Meachen Rau

 Blue Level: New ideas with a larger vocabulary and a variety
of language structures.

At the Beach by Patricia M. Stockland
The Playground Snake by Brian Moses

 Yellow Level: Challenging ideas with an expanded vocabulary
and a wide variety of sentences.

Flynn Flies High by Hilary Robinson
Marvin, the Blue Pig by Karen Wallace
Moo! by Penny Dolan
Pippin's Big Jump by Hilary Robinson
The Queen's Dragon by Anne Cassidy
Sounds Like Fun by Dana Meachen Rau
Tired of Waiting by Dana Meachen Rau
Whose Birthday Is It? by Sherryl Clark

 Green Level: More complex ideas with an extended vocabulary
range and expanded language structures.

Clever Cat by Karen Wallace
Flora McQuack by Penny Dolan
Izzie's Idea by Jillian Powell
Naughty Nancy by Anne Cassidy
The Princess and the Frog by Margaret Nash
The Roly-Poly Rice Ball by Penny Dolan
Run! by Sue Ferraby
Sausages! by Anne Adeney
Stickers, Shells, and Snow Globes by Dana Meachen Rau
The Truth About Hansel and Gretel by Karina Law
Willie the Whale by Joy Oades

A complete list of *Read-it!* Readers is available on our Web site:
www.picturewindowbooks.com